Pooh's Graduation

Printed in the United States of America

Library of Congress number: 00-108958
ISBN: 0-7364-1157-7 (paperback)

First Random House Edition: January 2001

www.randomhouse.com/kids/disney
www.disneybooks.com

DISNEY'S
A Winnie the Pooh First Reader

Pooh's Graduation

Isabel Gaines
Illustrated by Orlando de la Paz and Thompson Bros.

Random House 🏠 New York

One spring morning,
Winnie the Pooh and his friends
heard a very happy sound.
"Yippee!" someone shouted.

4

"That sounds like Christopher Robin,"
said Pooh.

Christopher Robin called out,

"I've just graduated from the first grade.

I got a diploma and an award, too!"

Everyone gathered around.

Owl read the medal,

"Best Reader in the First Grade."

"That's wonderful," said Pooh.

"But what does grad-u-at-ed mean?"

"It means that I have completed first grade," Christopher Robin said.

"I'm another year smarter."

"I want to graduate, too," said Pooh.

And Roo couldn't help asking,

"What's an award?"

"An award is a prize you win
for being the best at something,"
said Christopher Robin.

"Being the best at something
is awfully hard," said Eeyore glumly.
"It takes practice," said Owl.

11

Suddenly, Christopher Robin
had an idea.

"Let's have a graduation party,"
he said. "I will give out diplomas
to all of you."

"Can we get awards, too?" asked Roo.

"Of course," said Christopher Robin.

Christopher Robin got right to work.
He used colored paper and ribbon
to make awards and diplomas.

He even made a graduation cap
for each of his friends.

Everyone else was busy, too.

Owl was busy practicing giving speeches.

But he had no one to practice on,

until Pooh came along.

Kanga was busy baking cookies.

She needed Pooh to taste the dough

and make sure it was just right.

Roo was busy finger painting.

He asked Pooh to help him pick out
just the right picture.

As Pooh walked by Rabbit's garden,
Rabbit needed help finding
just the right carrot.

19

Pooh found Piglet

tangled up in kite string.

After unraveling him,

Pooh helped Piglet

find the best spot to fly his kite.

20

"Watch me bounce!" cried Tigger,

as Pooh wandered by.

Pooh gladly did.

Pooh met Eeyore on a bridge.

He helped him practice Pooh Sticks.

Pooh went back home.

He was very tired.

"I'll take a quick nap,"

said Pooh, "before I practice

what I am best at."

But when Pooh awoke,

it was time for the party!

Pooh hurried over

just as it began.

23

"I'll call your name,"
said Christopher Robin.
"And then you come up
to get your diploma
and your special award."

GRADUATION
TODAY

He called Owl up first.

"Owl, here is your diploma.

You get the award for

Best Speaker!"

"Thank you so much!" said Owl.

"This reminds me of the time

I won the award for Best Hoot."

Kanga won the award for

Best Cookie Maker.

Roo won for Best Finger Painting.

Rabbit got the award for Best Carrot.

And Piglet was given

the Best Kite-Flyer award.

28

Tigger won the Best Bounce award.

And Eeyore was given an award

for Best Pooh Sticks Player.

Pooh was very happy

for the awards his friends

were getting.

But he couldn't think

of anything he did the best.

"Finally," said Christopher Robin,

"the last award goes to Pooh,

for being the Best Friend

in the Hundred-Acre Wood!"

31

"Me?" said Pooh.
"I didn't think I was
the best at anything."

"Silly bear," said Christopher Robin.

"You are a best friend.

And here is your diploma

and your award to prove it."

"Happy graduation!"
said Christopher Robin.

Can you match the words with the
pictures?

diploma

award

cookies

kite

cap

Fill in the missing letters.

pi_ture

carro_

bou_ce

s_ick

thin_

Follow all the adventures
of Pooh and his friends!

Be Quiet, Pooh!

Bounce, Tigger, Bounce!

Eeyore Finds Friends

The Giving Bear

Happy Birthday, Eeyore!

Pooh and the Storm That Sparkled

Pooh Gets Stuck

Pooh's Best Friend

Pooh's Christmas Gifts

Pooh's Easter Egg Hunt